Eugene and The Magic Dagger

by Ezra Turner

Illustrated by Ira Pearman Philip III

Dedication

To my parents, Peter and Edith Trott
for their inspiration.
Many thanks to Mrs. Martha Vincent,
Mrs. Norma Scanlon and
Mr. GeOgre Wardman.

@ Copyright 2020
Ezra Turner

All rights reserved. No part of this book may be reproduced or utilized in any form or by any means, electronic or mechanical, including photocopying, recording or by any information storage and retrieval system, without permission in writing from the author.

ISBN: 978-0-947482-02-2

Table of Contents

1. The Adventures of Eugene 1
2. Gone but not Forgotten 12
3. Bermuda Triangle 15
4. Lost at Sea 20
5. Kadova 22
6. Monkey Island 26
7. Crow Island 31
8. Cockroach Island 34
9. Rabbit Island 38
10. Trunk Island 44

Eugene and the Magic Dagger

Harrington Sound
GOD'S COUNTRY

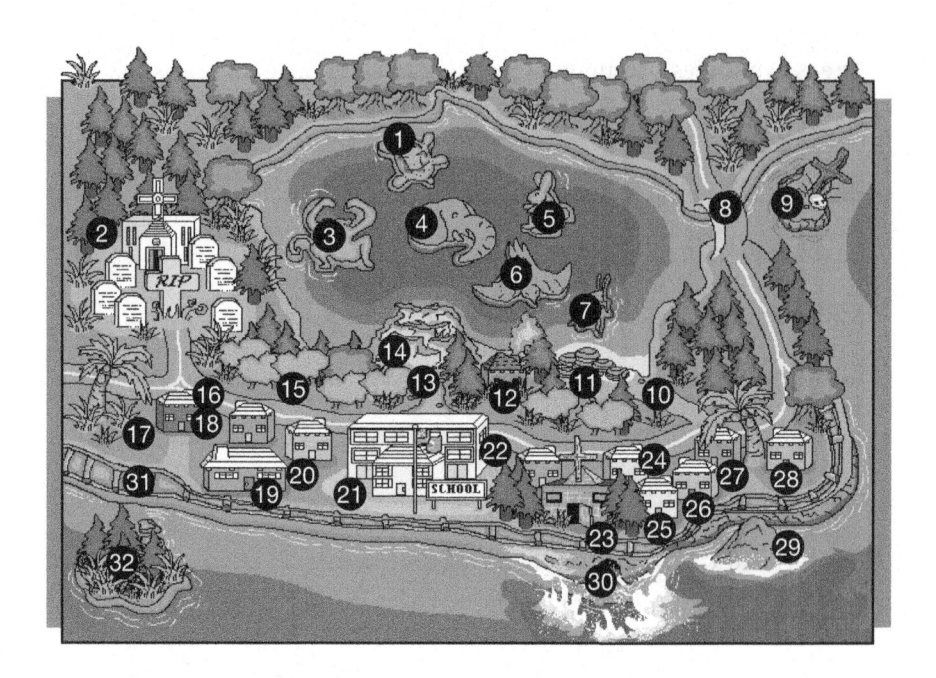

Key

1. Turtle Island
2. Trinity Church
3. Monkey Island
4. Trunk Island
5. Rabbit Island
6. Crow Island
7. Cockroach Island
8. Flatt's Bridge
9. Witch's Island
10. Path
11. Mussel Bay
12. Kadova's House
13. Rock Path
14. Abbot's Cliff
15. Cherry Land
16. Main Road
17. The Walkers' House
18. Dale's House
19. Wendel & Kate's House
20. Johnny's House
21. Francis Patton School
22. The Caseys' House
23. The Church
24. The Paynter House
25. The Davis' House
26. The Hill House
27. Eugene & David's House
28. Mr. Trotts' House
29. Davis Rock
30. Nell's Kitched
31. Railway Tracks
32. Bay Island

iv

The Adventures of Eugene

So powerful were the currents that rushed under Flatt's Bridge that they prevented powerboats from leaving Harrington Sound. On this particular day, the bridge was full of excited children surrounding a thirteen-year-old boy who was preparing to jump into the water. The exercise was forbidden; parents did not even allow their children to fish from the bridge. This thirteen-year-old boy was different, though. He was Eugene, the greatest athlete to come out of God's country, the name given to Hamilton Parish. The children practiced the game of "taking nerve." You might know it as "chicken."

Every summer, children from God's country jumped off cliffs of every height into deep and sometimes shallow water. They started from the Walker house in Bailey's Bay and reached the house of Mr. Trott, the postman. The winner's name was written in the record book for that year. Eugene was the only boy to win the competition three consecutive times. If he won this year, he would attain god-status among the children. Eugene wanted this honor more than anything, because he believed gods were immortal and could enter into the great city of Atlantis. The adventures of Eugene, as he prepared to go to Atlantis, took place in Bermuda a long time ago, when every day was a new adventure.

Since February, the longtails had been building their nests, and when summer arrived, the bird songs were music to everyone's ears.

Railway tracks separated the homes from the cliffs and ran for two miles between the Walker and Trott houses, bypassing Johnny's house. Then came Wendell and Kate's house, followed by Dale's house, before Francis Patton School. The tracks then came to the Casey house. Mrs. Casey taught music and had introduced everyone in the parish to music. Between the Casey house and that of a popular teacher named Miss Paynter sat a grey church surrounded by beautiful cedar trees. Opposite the church, on the other side of the tracks, was a cave called Nell's Kitchen. Then came the Davis House, and opposite it was Davis Rock, followed by the Hill home. Mr. Hill taught carpentry to the local children. Eugene's house was next door to his. An acre of land separated Eugene's house and Mr. Trott's home. Opposite that, on the shore side, was a cove that protected small boats from the rough seas.

Everybody knew everybody, and children from almost every household participated in the summer event. Eugene was busy preparing himself. David, his younger brother, tried to help out, but all Eugene needed was a listening ear for all his stories. He kept repeating one story, the tale of Atlantis.

It was a place where gods went and never hungered or died. The streets were paved with gold, and gods lived in harmony. He told other stories of catching the Russian wind and the magic dagger, which he needed, to enter Atlantis. He knew the entrance to Atlantis was in Harrington Sound, where the currents began and ended. Some called it Devil's Hole.

When the day finally arrived, all the children met on the rocky cliffs opposite the Walker house. From Mr. Walker's house to the church, the cliffs were no more than six feet high, but the water was only two to three feet deep. The rules stated that if anyone touched a reef or the bottom, he was disqualified. Usually, by the time the competition reached Nell's Kitchen, only two boys remained.

On this day, just before Davis Rock, four boys remained: Dale, Johnny, Eugene, and Wendell. Johnny jumped from the rock first, a fifteen-foot drop into three feet of water. Trying to impress everyone, he did two flips as he dove. He did not finish the second flip and hit the bottom headfirst. The children let out a sigh of relief, followed by laughter, when he resurfaced quickly, holding his head.

Wendell was too cautious. His shallow dive caused him to come up too quickly, and his feet touched the bottom. The crowd booed and laughed as Wendell joined Johnny. Next came Dale. He sprang, touched his toes in a key position and made a perfect dive. He surfaced and shouted, "Yes!" Cheers rang out.

Eugene walked up to the rock and looked across at Nell's Kitchen before jumping. He glanced down at his dagger, the dagger that belonged to the Evil Ogre, who everyone believed lived in Nell's Kitchen. Eugene needed to use his dagger to defeat death, before

Eugene and the Magic Dagger

entering Atlantis. Eugene thought about his battle with the Evil Ogre for the dagger.

The night had been rainy, no stars or moon to light the way, as Eugene paced along the railway track to Nell's Kitchen. The bank side leading to the cave was muddy, and Eugene had to crawl on his hands and knees to keep from slipping. When he reached the entrance, the cave was too dark for him to see inside. He carefully climbed in anyway, feeling around in the dark until he found a big rock to hide behind. After he waited a few hours lightening flashed and lit up the cave. The ground rumbled as the Evil-Ogre entered the cave on his side was the magic dagger, that was glowing red. The Ogre set on the huge bolder that Eugene was hiding behind, he let out a loud roar, Eugene's hair stood on end, while he watched the evil Ogre stretched his huge arms before he removed the Magic dagger form his side and placed the dargger by his enormoue feet. The dagger's glow began to fade

Eugene knew it was now or never. He leapt forward, gripped the magic dagger, and quickly scrambled out of the cave, running up the bank side onto the railway tracks. The Evil Ogre hooves clopped behind Eugene as he raced toward home. Just as he reached home, he heard a pitifull scream and turned to see the Evil Ogre fading from sight.

Back on the cliff, Eugene raised his hands above his head. He knew this dive was important. All the kids stood speechless as Eugene sprang into the air, floated down, cut through the surface of the water, resurfaced, and raised his fists to the cheers from God's children.

From Davis Rock to Eugene's home, the cliffs were high and the water deep. The trip back gave Eugene and Dale time to perform several acrobatic jumps for the crowd, which cheered with joy. The fun stopped when the group reached Eugene's house. This cliff was forty feet high, and below it was a twentyfoot-high pyramid-shaped rock. Divers had to jump over the rock before landing in the ocean.

Dale was the first to jump. He backed away from the edge before he took a running dive. He glided in the air and came down directly toward the large rock. The kids held their breath. Some closed their eyes. They all screamed, and Dale missed the rock by inches before safely entering the ocean. Eugene made his way to the edge, then took ten paces backwards. About two strides into his run, he slipped and tumbled over the edge, heading straight toward the large rock. Everyone gasped and ran to the edge of the cliff, just in time to witness a gust of wind that blew Eugene over and away from the rock. Most of the children rubbed their eyes in disbelief. When Eugene resurfaced, he glanced toward Bay Island, where he had trapped the

Eugene and the Magic Dagger

Russian wind in a little glass bottle, sealed with a cork.

The Russian wind was the first and last of the winds that occur once a month at the center of the Earth. Eugene said Bay Island was the center of the Earth. Cedar trees and aloe hid a perfect little pink-sand beach on the island.

Eugene needed the Russian wind to open the door of Atlantis. The story that Eugene told was unbelievable, but true.

The moon was full and the stars shone brightly as Eugene made his way along the railway tracks. He picked up his pace and clutched the magic dagger, while passing Nell's Kitchen. He did not stop until he reached the Walker home, where he had to wade and swim across seventy-five yards of ocean to reach the island.

While swimming, he collided with a big manta ray. The manta ray turned and whipped Eugene with his tail. Eugene grabbed for the magic dagger and, when the manta ray attacked again, Eugene held the magic dagger above his head. The manta ray swam away, flapping its mighty fins with fear and in pain. Eugene hurriedly swam to the island, where he picked fresh aloe and applied it to his wound. He made his way along the little pink beach toward the top of the island, where he sat amid the cedar trees, counting the stars. Exactly on his two-thousandth star, he heard a loud noise, like a kettle boiling. Eugene jumped to his feet, took the little glass bottle from his pocket, removed the cork, and held the bottle in the air. The bottle vibrated uncontrollably, as the Russian wind filled it, but Eugene managed to replace the cork, and the vibration and noise stopped. When Eugene tried to move, he felt like he was falling and falling. Eventually he awoke the next morning to the rising sun, the bottle still in his hand.

The Adventures of Eugene

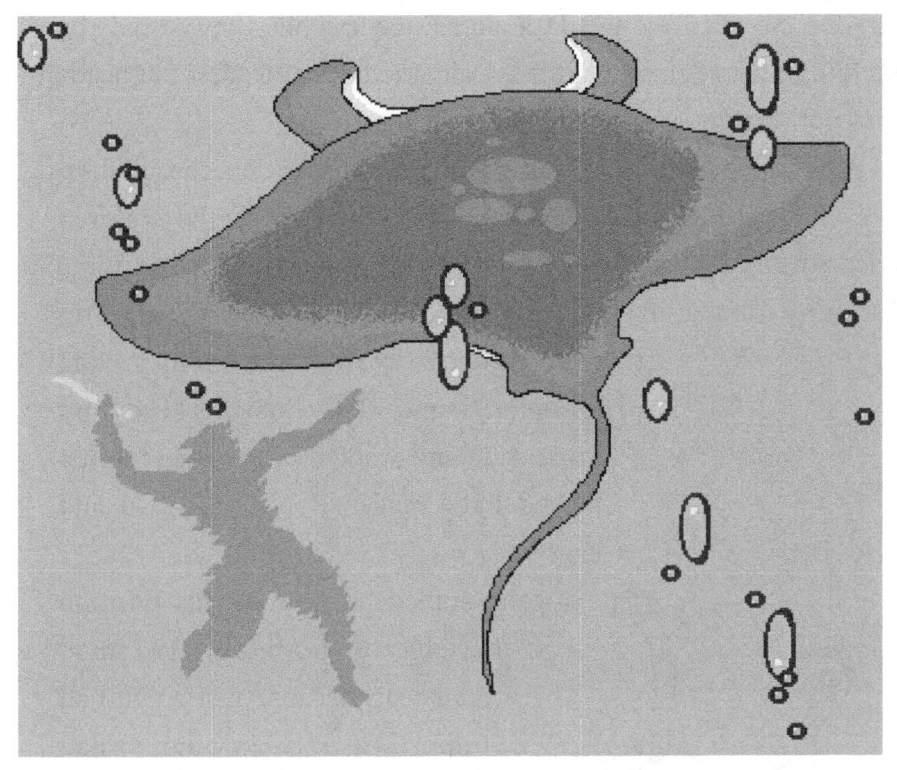

Back on the tracks, Dale and Eugene, followed by the excited children, made their way to the last and final cliff opposite Mr. Trott's house. The cliff was thirty feet high, with six feet of water below. The only jump to take, to prevent hitting the bottom, was a jump called "Belly Buster." You had to jump with limp arms and legs and land on your belly, which usually knocked the breath out of you.

Dale walked to the edge and took a deep breath. When he jumped, though, he flapped his arms and legs, instead of going limp. His belly hit the water and sounded like an explosion. When he resurfaced, he was barely able to raise his fists to God's children. Eugene walked to the edge and dove in the perfect "Belly Buster" position. He hit the water with half the splash Dale had made. The kids whooped with excitement. Draws did not exist; someone had to win.

7

Eugene and the Magic Dagger

Everyone crowded around Dale and Eugene while they tossed the coin into the air. Before it landed, Dale cried out, "Heads!" But heads it was not. Eugene smiled. "I choose Flatt's Bridge."

Although a jump from Flatt's Bridge was forbidden, the children got excited and shouted, "Yes!" At Flatt's Bridge, all the children circled around Dale at the edge of the bridge as he prepared to jump. His skinny frame quivered all over. He stared at the rising current, strong enough to stop a motorboat from leaving Harrington Sound. Dale shook his head from side to side and walked away. The children clucked like chickens, as if they had laid eggs.

Eugene smiled as he took his position on the edge of the bridge. He stood without fear, because just as he had trapped the Russian wind, he had also trapped Fear in his little glass bottle.

Before he dove off the bridge, he reflected on the night he had trapped Fear. A heavy mist hid the full moon. Eugene made his way down the railway tracks to the Walker house, his bottle safely in his pocket. He crossed the main road onto Trinity Church Road, which led to Trinity Church. Eugene believed Fear lived there.

When he reached the church, it looked ghostly. He made his way over the tombstones and up onto the hillside, where he sat and looked at the shadowy church. It resembled a haunted house, with the ghostly water of Harrington

Sound in the background. Every now and again, he heard the howl of stray dogs in the neighborhood.

Eugene saw a little girl, playing with her doll, on a gravestone in front of him. He rubbed his eyes and opened them wider, before he got the courage to speak. "Hi," he whispered, but the girl acted as if he were not there. Eugene repeated himself several times, but she ignored him. He walked over, reached out to her, and said, "I'm talking to you." The little girl dropped her doll and backed away, her mouth gaping as if she had seen a ghost.

"I am not going to hurt you," Eugene assured her. The little girl struggled to speak. "You can see me?" "Of course," Eugene replied. "I am not blind."

She turned and ran toward the church. Eugene watched while hundreds of people poured out of the church, led by the little girl. Eugene tried to run, but his feet would not move. The crowd made its way up the hill and sat around Eugene. The little girl pointed. "He can see us."

One of the men said, "That's impossible. We see them, but they cannot see us." He reached out to touch Eugene. The man gasped when Eugene pulled away. The little girl spoke again. "I told you, he can see us." One of the old men said, "My name is Percy. What's your name?" Eugene stammered his name and asked in the same breath, "What are you all doing here?" Percy smiled. "I should be asking you that question, because we live here. You see, Eugene, we are all dead." Eugene wanted to run, but his feet still would not move. His hair stood on end.

The man continued, "We are trapped by Fear, who guards the gates. We long to be reunited with our loved ones, but everyone is afraid of Fear."

Eugene and the Magic Dagger

The little girl dropped to her knees in front of Eugene. "Please help us."

A little old lady said, "Hush, girl. What can a mere boy do, when we run at the sight of Fear and hide?" As she finished, a rush of wind blew. All the dead ran to the church and slammed the door behind them.

Eugene's eyes searched the gravesite. His heart pounded as he sensed Fear coming toward him. He felt something he had never felt before, as if he were afraid of himself.

Eugene wiggled the little glass bottle from his pocket, removed the cork, and stretched his hand up in the air. Fear let out a loud, spine-tingling scream as the Russian wind sucked it into the bottle. Eugene sealed the bottle with the cork. The mist cleared; the moon appeared, surrounded by twinkling stars. When the moon shone on the church, the doors flew open and, one by one, the people ran out. They jumped over the gate and shouted, "We're free! We're free!"

The little girl made her way toward the gate, turned to Eugene, and said quietly, "Thank you."

The shouts of the children awakened Eugene from his daydreaming. "Jump! Jump!" Eugene took a deep breath and got ready to make the final jump that would put him in the record books as a god.

Only his little brother David knew what was going to happen next, and he promised Eugene he would never tell, because Eugene promised him he would return from Atlantis once a year and put a gold coin in their special place, in a jar buried two feet underneath the Royal Poinciana in their back yard. David held back his tears as Eugene dove into the rushing currents below. They swallowed him up, and only David knew where Eugene had gone. He swam to Atlantis, the city paved with gold, where gods go and never die.

Eugene never broke the promise; once a year, David found a gold coin hidden in the special place. Also, people have told many stories about being saved at sea by a boy who wore a dagger on his side that glowed in the dark.

Gone but not Forgotten

In big letters, the first page of the newspaper read "Miracle." The article said "...two nine-year-old boys, Terry and David had been lost fishing near Nell's Kitchen three days earlier."

The police and everyone from God's country searched every cave along the seashore, from the Walker house to Mr. Trott's house, without finding a trace of the boys. Divers searched every underwater cave, with no success. All hopes vanished, and after a search of two days, the search party was called off, leaving all of God's family from God's country and the whole island bewildered.

On the third day, though, a miracle happened. A fisherman passing Bay Island heard a child's cries for help. When he went to rescue the child, he was stunned to recognize the little boy as David, one of the boys who had been missing. He was taken to the hospital where he was found to be in perfect condition. He was happy to see his parents and

Gone but not Forgotten

hugged them with glee. The story he told the police and his parents was more astonishing than the disappearance of the boys.

He said while he and Terry were fishing, they kept hearing a noise coming from nell's Kitchen. The boys became frightened and ran, but Terry got tangled in his fishing line at the exact moment a big fish took his line and pulled him into the ocean. David jumped into the water and tried his best to untangle Terry, but the fish pulled both of them deep below the ocean and into a reef. The line finally snapped from rubbing against the sharp coral. Before the boys could rise to the surface, a strong current sucked them into an underwater cave. David fell unconscious, and later awoke in the most beautiful cave he had ever seen. Enormous stalactites and stalagmites decorated it. Terry lay on his stomach a few feet away. David went over and shook him several times, but Terry did not move; he had drowned. David cried, but soon he heard a voice behind him saying, "Don't cry. We all must die to live."

David turned around and behind him stood Eugene, his skinny body covered only with a pair of shorts. On his side, the Magic dagger glowed. David ran into Eugene's arms, and when Eugene held him, David felt his body renewing itself with joyful energy.

Eugene walked over to Terry, picked him up and said to David, "Follow me." He walked through the cave, and the stalactites and stalagmites played a sweet song. The boys came to an opening, where the rays of the sun reflected every color of the rainbow. From the heavens, gold steps came down. David and Eugene, carrying Terry, ascended the steps. When they reached the top, a huge door swung

Eugene and the Magic Dagger

open. David saw castles and streets of gold. Huge trees talked to each other. He was so taken with the beauty of the place that he barely noticed that Eugene had put Terry down. When David looked at Terry, he smiled back, quite alive. David shrieked with joy, and both boys embraced.

David stayed for two days and met many of the people he had heard about in Sunday School. On the third day, Eugene told David he must leave, but that Terry could never leave again or return to life as humans knew it. Eugene said Terry would be safe in Atlantis. Both boys and Eugene hugged. Before David knew it, he was on Bay Island sitting on the little pink beach. David said Terry sent his love to everyone and wanted to let his family know he was happy, and if they stay as special to the world as they were to him, he would meet them at the entrance of Atlantis, when their special day of rest came.

Bermuda Triangle

One day Wendell and his sister Kate were fishing in their little boat about a half mile northeast of Bay Island, when the ocean opened up a big hole, which turned into a waterfall. The strong current pulled the boat over the edge. Wendell and Kate fell out of the boat and yelled for help. The next thing Kate remembered, she was awakening and gazing around in a daze. All around her were large ships, little boats, and airplanes, all in good condition. When she looked up, instead of seeing the sky, she saw the ocean, as if some force were stopping it from falling on her. Out of the corner of her eye, Kate saw Wendell. She ran to him and shook him. Water flowed out of his mouth, and he coughed up water for about two minutes, before Kate could help him to his feet.

Wendell looked around. "Where are we?"

Kate replied, "I don't know. All I know is that we're not dead."

"Are you sure? Everything I see looks dead." Wendell saw a huge shark swimming above his head, and he jumped back.

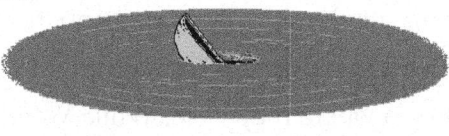

Kate patted her brother on the shoulder. "Don't worry. Neither he or the water can come through. It's like we're in an empty fish tank with water all around us."

Wendell nodded, "Let's take a look in those ships and planes and see what we can find."

When they walked around one of the ships, they found skeletons that looked as if they were frozen in time. Kate and Wendell held onto each other tightly as they walked throughout the ship. When they came to the kitchen, they found plenty of canned food. Wendell said, "At least we won't go hungry."

Kate's eyes teared up. "How can you talk about food?"

"Kate, we can't help those other people; they're dead. But we can help ourselves, and maybe we can find a way out of this place. I think we need as much strength as possible."

Kate stopped crying. "You're right. Let's see what else we can make use of." Together they found flashlights and all kinds of useful things.

They spent the night aboard the ship. Some time in the early morning, Kate awoke to see a figure, which vanished when she tried to focus on it. She rocked Wendell awake. "I saw someone," she whispered.

Wendell got a flashlight, and they both looked around. After an hour of looking, Wendell said, "You must have been dreaming."

Kate shook her head. "I swear I saw someone."

When they left the ship, the sun shone through the water and made rainbows. The two spent the whole day looking through the ships and airplanes. They found only skeletons, no sign of life, and no clue to where they were. While Wendell wandered through one of the airplanes, Kate sat outside on a big rock and watched the fish eating and playing. One of the fish stopped and stared back at her. She moved her head from side to side, and the fish moved its head from side to side. Kate stood and walked, and the fish followed her. She paused and put her hand on her chin.

"My name is Kate. What's yours?"

The fish said, "My name is Sally." Kate screamed, "The fish can talk!" and ran to Wendell.

"Calm down, Kate. Now tell me slowly what happened."

After Kate had told him, Wendell laughed, "First it's a ghost, and now it's a talking fish."

Kate gripped his hand and pulled him. "Just follow me." Wendell obeyed. He folded his arms while Kate looked at the fish and said, "My name is Kate. What's yours?"

The fish blew bubbles.

Wendell laughed, turned around, and walked back toward the airplane.

Kate cried.

The fish said, "Why are you crying?"

Wendell stopped in his tracks, turned around, and saw the fish laughing.

Kate laughed too. "I told you the fish could talk!" Wendell rushed back to his sister's side. "Ask the fish if she knows Eugene."

Sally answered, "Of course, I know Eugene. He is the protector of God's children."

Wendell raised his voice. "Tell Eugene we need his help."

Sally swam away. She moved through the underwater caves that led into Harrington Sound, where she was greeted by a dolphin.

Sally told him Wendell and Kate were trapped in the Bermuda Triangle. The dolphin swiftly swam to Eugene and relayed the message.

Eugene and the Magic Dagger

Eugene knew the only way out was through the Valley of the Dragons. Eugene jumped on the dolphin's back, and they swam to the entrance of the Bermuda Triangle, where Eugene dove into it. Kate and Wendell were seated on a rock, when Eugene appeared. They squealed with delight. They followed Eugene to the opening of the Bermuda Triangle, a deep valley surrounded by huge trees.

Wendell asked, "What is this place?"

Eugene replied, "It's the Valley of the Dragons." He told them to stay where they were, and he walked through the entrance holding the magic dagger high above his head.

Several dragons lumbered out. One of them shouted, "So you're Eugene, the protector of God's children." He laughed and breathed fire at Eugene, who nipped behind a large rock, to prevent himself from being roasted.

Before the dragon could breathe his fire again, Eugene jumped on his tail, ran up his back, and pierced him in the neck with the magic dagger. The dragon let out a loud groan and fell to the ground.

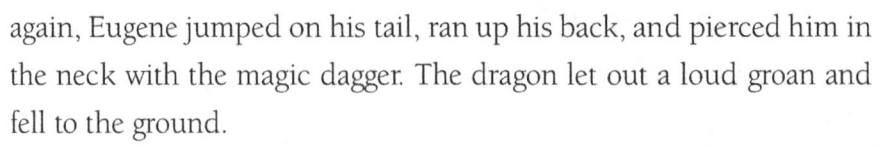

Eugene leapt off the dragon's back, but one of the other dragons swiped him with his tail and threw him twenty feet. He hit the ground and lay helpless. All the dragons laughed as they got ready to shoot flames at him. Kate drew their attention, though. She ran toward Eugene. When she reached him, he told her to push her hand through his side and find the little glass bottle. He assured her he would not feel anything. She did as he wished and felt around until she found it.

Eugene said, "Quick, pull out the cork!"

When she did, Fear screeched with joy at being released. The dragons ran and buried their heads at the sight of Fear.

Wendell joined Eugene and Kate and helped Eugene to his feet. The three walked through the Valley of the Dragons to the other side. With Eugene's strength restored, he turned and faced the dragons with the Magic dagger in one hand and the bottle in the other. Fear screamed as the Russian wind sucked it back into the bottle. Eugene quickly sealed the vessel and thanked Kate and Wendell.

The next thing the children remembered, was being back in their boat on top of the ocean. They quickly rowed back to land.

Eugene and the Magic Dagger

Lost at Sea

One day, Wendell and Dale were fishing a half mile off land when the air swiftly grew cool. Clouds rolled over and over themselves, as if in a race. The boys rowed toward shore as fast as they could, but the current became stronger than ever, and the wind blew so hard the boys had to hold on for their lives. The cold weather lasted five minutes and then stopped as suddenly as it started. The boys searched the horizon for land, but all they saw was ocean as far as the eye could see. Night came quickly, and the stars appeared one by one, twinkling on the dark, lonely ocean.

Wendell called out, "What's that?" He pointed at a bright light coming toward them.

Dale answered, "It's a ship!" Both boys screamed for help, but the loud ship engine blocked out their cries for help. The vessel slipped past them by thirty feet, and in its wake rocked the little boat from side to side. The boys scrambled to keep the boat afloat. In a few minutes, the sea was calm again. They held each other tightly throughout the night, to keep warm.

The next day, squawks of seagulls awakened the boys. The day droned on, long and hot, and they grew thirsty. When the sun finally set, the temperature dropped, and the boys shivered again. The sky was so dark, they couldn't see a star. To make matters worse, the sky lit up with jagged flashes of lightning, followed by loud claps of thunder. They cried and held each other. The rain fell in buckets all night. The boys bailed water out of the boat, but the more they poured out, the more it rained. Their muscles grew weak, and their arms became tired. They stopped to rest and sleep, and sometime in the early morning, the boat sank. The boys floated in the cold water and held onto each other as they drifted along with the current. They were thankful to see the sun rise.

Dale pointed at a silver fin coming directly toward them. A huge shark stopped two feet in front of them. He made a swift turn and splashed the boys. Both boys gasped for air. Just as they caught their breath, they saw the shark coming toward them at a fast speed. He tilted on his side and opened his mouth to bite them.

They shut their eyes an screamed. They heard a loud bump, and they felt themselves swirling as the ocean turned into a whirlpool. It stopped, and the boys opened their eyes, to find Eugene, riding a dolphin. He took the boys safely back to the island.

Kadova

Wendell, Dale, and Johnny were part of a club called "The Invisibles." To become a member of the club, they had to steal one of Kadova's silver coins. Merely the mention of the name of Kadova sent chills down the spines of the bravest of God's children.

Kadova lived in an old limestone house that stood amid cedar and spice trees on ten acres of land otherwise dominated by cherry trees. Eugene called it Cherryland. The biggest red cherries grew on Kadova's trees, and after school, God's children crossed the street opposite Francis Patton School, where they were greeted with sweet cherries. From there a rocky road led all the way to Abbot's Cliff that overlooked Harrington Sound, or "Devil's Hole," as God's children called it.

God's children were always on the lookout for Kadova. No one had ever seen him, but the screams coming from Cherryland often sent them running for their lives. He was described many ways: Some said he was half dog and half man; others said he was half boar and half man. He supposedly had a treasure of silver coins to tempt the children.

The Adventures of Eugene

One day, Wendell's sister Kate declared she wanted to join the club and would go steal a silver coin from Kadova. The boys laughed, even though Kate was as tough as some of the boys. They knew that no other boy would take the test, much less a girl. Kate insisted, though, and because several boys gathered around, The Invisibles took up her challenge.

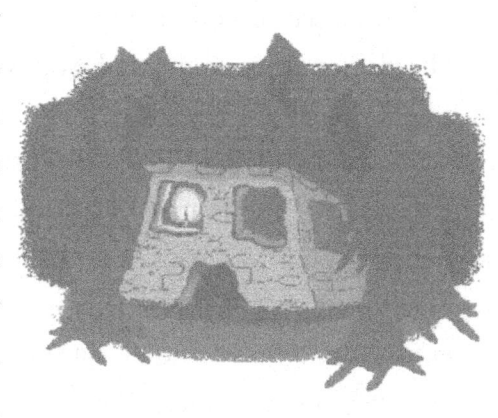

Dale said, "Okay, Kate, here's the deal. Tonight you'll go to Kadova's house and steal one silver coin. To make sure you don't trick us, we'll walk with you to the entrance of Cherryland and wait for you to return . . . if you ever do return." The boys laughed.

Kate put her hands on her hips. "Okay, I'll see you all tonight." The boys giggled until she was out of sight. Dale asked,

"Wendell, is your sister serious?"

Wendell nodded. "I'm afraid to say she is very serious."

Later Wendell pleaded with Kate not to put herself to the test, but he had no success.

That night as Kate walked down the railway tracks followed by several of God's children, Wendell, Dale, and Johnny tried their best to scare Kate. Each told her scary tales about Kadova. They reached Francis Patton School, crossed the road and entered Cherryland. About fifty yards down on the dark path, they stopped. Wendell told Kate, "We'll wait here for you."

23

"Okay. I'll see you on my return."

She walked through the dark and sometimes had to feel her way, when her eyes could not see.

God's children followed her at a distance.

Kate spotted the flames of a candle and followed the light off the path for about fifty yards, until she came upon Kadova's house. The limestone house had no windows or doors, just big holes where the windows and doors should have been. The roof was black from weather and bird droppings. When Kate came closer, she noticed several candles burning.

She climbed through the hole in the wall where the door should have been. Her eyes searched the room. It had the biggest bed she had ever seen. "Kadova, whatever you are, you must be huge," she whispered. Candles flickered high in every corner. Two candles a black and a red one sat on a little table in the center of the room. Kate searched the room for coins. She looked on the table. She got down on her knees and stretched her hand under the bed. She put her hand in farther, and touched something. She yanked her hand out, but heard the jingling sound of coins. She reached back under the bed and found a little pouch. As she was pulling it out, a hairy hand gripped her by the wrist. Kate screamed so loud that God's children, who were still nearby, turned and ran home. Her screams echoed throughout Cherryland. She pleaded, but the hairy hand did not let her go. Instead it tried to drag her under the bed.

Out of nowhere, a loud voice boomed, "Kadova!" and the hand instantly released Kate. She jumped up and turned around to find herself face to face with Eugene, who held the magic dagger high above his head. She ran to him and hugged him. The next thing Kate knew, she was home, sitting in the center of her bedroom floor.

By that time, God's children were climbing the stairs to Kate's house. All the kids called out to Kate's mother. She opened the door and stood speechless, while the kids circled her, chattering, stammering, and blabbering. When she finally found words, she said, "Hush! One at a time, please."

Wendell said, "You've got to come quick! Kadova is eating Kate." His mother looked puzzled. "All of you go home, because you almost scared the life out of me with your silly prank."

Wendell begged. Tears ran down his face.

Wendell's mother shook her head. "Your sister is in her room." All the kids ran to Kate's room and opened the door. Kate was sitting with her back to them. When they shouted her name, she stood, turned around, and opened her hands. They were filled with silver coins.

Monkey Island

Harrington Sound is scattered with little islands, such as Monkey Island, Cockroach Island, Turtle Island, Rabbit Island, Trunk Island, and Crow Island. Each island has its story. On Trunk Island lived the wicked goblin; on Turtle Island lived the giant turtle; on Rabbit Island lived killer rabbits; on Crow Island lived flesh-eating crows, and on Cockroach Island lived thousands of cockroaches. On Monkey Island, lived a mad scientist who used monkeys for his experiments. No one knew what he was up to. All they knew was that throughout the night, the monkeys screamed, as if in great pain.

The Invisibles, plus one girl, decided they would go to the island and find out what the mad scientist was doing. The nearest point to Monkey Island was opposite Trinity Church, and there was a 100-yard swim before they reached the island. The Invisibles, plus one girl, met on the railway track as the sun set. All of them wore scarves tied around their heads and carried flashlights. They made their way down the railway track to the Walker house, where they crossed the street to Trinity Church Road.

When they reached the church, they could see Monkey Island. They entered the water and began to swim.

Even though the moon was full and the stars shone brightly, the clouds always hung in Harrington Sound and gave it a ghostly appearance. Halfway across the water, they could hear the monkey screams, followed by shouts probably from the wicked goblin from Trunk Island. Even the giant turtle sounded off like a trumpet. The killer rabbits joined in, grinding their teeth.

The children plowed faster through the water. When they reached the island, loud shrieks came from the top of Abbot's Cliff. They recognized the voice and it was Kadova, jumping up and down, yelling at the top of his voice.

The kids were frightened, but their curiosity was stronger. Dale, leading the way, searched the island. Wendell said, "The sounds from the monkeys seem to be coming from underground."

Kate asked, "What's this?" she shone her flashlight on a handle. Johnny pulled on it, and a trap door opened. Rope steps led down. The Invisibles, plus one girl, challenged each other to determine who would go down first, with no success, so they drew straws. Kate was the unlucky one. She climbed down the ladder. When she reached the bottom, she heard the screams from the monkeys even louder. She flashed her light around and saw hundreds of jars filled with animal parts. "Yech!" she exclaimed, and the Invisibles all climbed down the rope ladder to find Kate. She pointed at the jars and held her hand over her mouth.

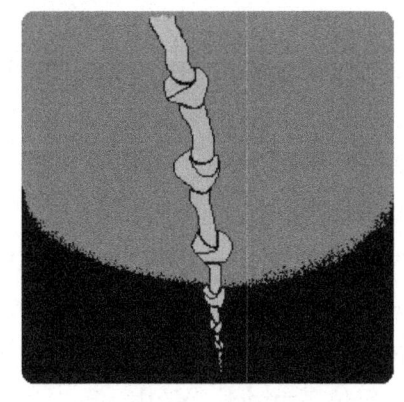

Dale groaned. "Gross! He really is a mad scientist."

Wendell roared, "Let's get out of here, before he finds us, and we wind up in jars."

The sorrowful cries from the monkeys touched Kate's heart. Instead of leaving, she walked farther into the underground cave. The Invisibles followed her, one by one. She came to a junction in the cave that had seven different paths. The kids listened carefully and took the tunnel from which the clamor was coming. A little way down the trail, they came to a huge room lit by hundreds of candles. They slowly walked toward the entrance, and the shrill sounds of the monkeys got louder when they entered. One little monkey in a cage jumped up and down. Kate opened the pen. The monkey sprang into her arms, hugged her, and calmed down.

Kate stroked the animal. "Poor little fellow. We're going to get you out of this place."

Johnny whooped. "What's that shining light?"

Two monkeys sagged limp and lifeless, strapped to separate chairs. Wires connected strange devices on their heads. The children turned around to run, but found themselves facing the mad scientist, who stood at the entrance. His long hair hung down his shoulders.

His face had a rough beard, and his big teeth glowed yellow-green.

He grinned. With a cackling voice, he said, "Now what have we got here? Just when I had finally given up, faith has given me a second chance." He took the monkey from Kate and tied up the children.

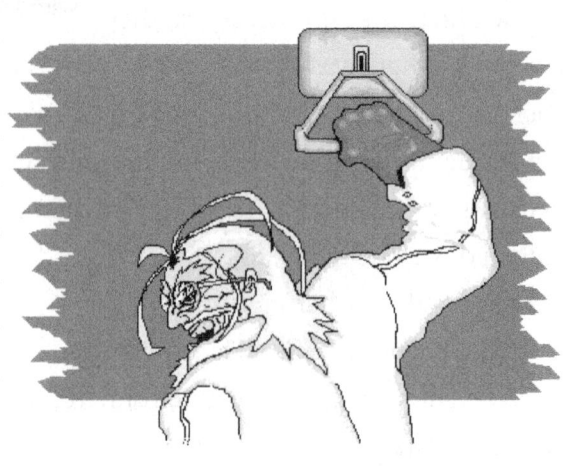

The Adventures of Eugene

He pushed the dead monkeys off the chairs. Their bodies fell to the ground. He strapped the little monkey into one of the chairs and put the device on his head. He turned to the quaking children. "Which of you wants to be the first to experience life's greatest experiment?"

The Invisibles, plus one girl, all bawled, "Not I!"

The mad scientist rubbed his chin. He looked at Kate. "You seem to be very fond of the monkey; you will be first." He reached out, gripped her, and strapped her into the chair. Kate cried for her life. He settled the device on her head and flipped a switch. The mad scientist clenched his fists and watched with excitement. His eyes grew wider, when Kate's and the monkey's bodies vibrated. They stopped and sat lifeless. He quickly cut off the switch and hung his head. He turned and looked at the Invisibles. "It looks like I failed again."

Tears filled the boys eyes. They heard a loud shriek, and when the mad scientist turned around, he saw it was coming from Kate, but she sounded like a monkey. He looked at the monkey, whose eyes were opening. The monkey's mouth formed the words. "What happened?" The Mad Scientist bubbled with joy. "It worked!" He laughed so loud he didn't hear the thunder. He stopped cluckling when a flash of lightning lit up the cave. He slowly rotated around to see Eugene, holding the magic dagger above his head. The mad scientist dropped to his knees and pleaded. "No! Don't stop me, now. I've waited all my life for this moment.

Eugene said, "You evil man." His eyes glowed.

The mad scientist jumped to his feet and ran into one of the tunnels. A big rock fell down and sealed him forever.

29

Eugene put one hand on the monkey and the other on Kate, and they became themselves again.

Kate jumped into Eugene's arms.

"Thank you! Thank you," she cooed.

Eugene freed the Invisibles, and as he was about to say farewell, Kate asked, "What about the monkey?"

Eugene smiled. "He will be welcome to live in Atlantis; that is, if he doesn't mind becoming a Golden Monkey."

The Invisibles, plus one girl, laughed.

Crow Island

David, Eugene's brother, awoke early. He looked out of his window to see the rays of the first sun. He quickly dressed and made his way to the Poinciana tree that grew in his back yard. Today was his tenth birthday, and Eugene always left David a gold coin in the jar buried about ten feet from the tree. When David reached the tree, he stopped. His eyes grew wide, and his mouth dropped open. The jar lay open on top of the ground, surrounded by soil. He ran to it, looked inside, and saw that the coins were gone. David almost cried, but before the first tear formed, he saw a big black feather. He stooped, picked it up, and examined it. It belonged to a crow, but it had little gold spots splattered around the tips of the feather, and David knew the theft was not the work of a normal crow. It was the work of the flesh-eating crow that lived on Crow Island, an area full of tall casuarina trees in Harrington Sound. If he was ever going to get his coins back, David would have to wait until nightfall when the crows were asleep and leave from the bottom of Abbot's Cliff, the closest point of land.

Rain fell, that evening, and the wind blew so hard the tips of the tall trees almost touched the ground. David, with only his flashlight to illuminate his way, wandered along the railway track. When he passed Nell's Kitchen, he heard the Evil Ogre huffing and puffing. He ran all the way to Francis Patton School, where he crossed the road and entered Cherryland. As he walked along the rocky path that led to Abbot's Cliff, the fearsome wind whistled and shook the trees. Cherries, rattled from their stems, fell and splattered David in the face. When he passed Kadova's house, a hairy hand reached out and gripped David's wrist. David's hair stood on end.

Luckily, he had oiled himself, and his little wrist slipped free. Faster than ever, he ran to Abbot's Cliff. He quickly climbed down the rocky path to the right of the cliff until he reached the bottom. The current was strong, and he had to swim strongly to reach the island.

When he arrived, the tall causarina trees rustled forcefully from side to side. David struggled up several trees to look for nests. He held on tightly, to keep from being blown off. When he found a nest, he carefully put his hand under the crow and felt around for his coins, but the only thing he found were eggs. Eventually he spotted a huge nest with the biggest crow he had ever seen sitting on it. He reached out, slowly put his hand under her, and felt around the nest. He heard a jingle and then felt coins. He collected them all, but when he tried to withdraw his hand, something pinched his hand. Quickly he yanked back, still holding the coins, and slid down the tree.

The crow cried out, followed by several calls from other crows. David swam like a speedboat back to the mainland. He climbed to the top of the cliff, then ran along the path. He heard the crows above him, their calls shrill. They darted around and dove toward him. David swung his arms above his head to stop the crows from pecking his head. He stumbled and fell over something in the path. He turned and shone his flashlight to see what tripped him.

Hairy arms reached out at him.

David sprang to his feet and ran so fast that he left a trail of smoke. When he reached the end of the path, he zipped across the street to Francis Patton School. He ran along the railway tracks, oblivious of several crows that perched on the school roof.

The birds flew down and dove at him as he ran toward home, with his coins still clutched safely in his hand.

Cockroach Island

Almost all of God's children crawled around on their hands and knees, turning over every rock in their path, searching for the biggest and fastest cockroaches they could find. The next day, the race of the cockroaches would draw children for miles, and God's children wanted to be ready for the big event.

While most of the children collected cockroaches during the day, the Invisibles, plus one girl, prepared themselves for the hunt that evening. They planned to win the race, and they knew where the biggest and fastest cockroaches lived, but the group had to wait until night to catch the bugs, because during the day, they hid deep in the earth.

When evening came, the Invisibles, plus one girl, walked down the railway tracks toward Mr. Trott's house, the shortest route to Cockroach Island. The kids had to cross the street and walk along a rocky path with cedar and spice trees on every side, until they reached Mussel Bay. Cockroach Island was fifty yards offshore, and it prevented strong currents from entering the little bay. Before the Invisibles, plus one girl, entered the shallow water, Johnny said, "I hope we don't wake

The Adventures of Eugene

Mussel Man" Mussel Man lived under the reefs. He fed on mussels, and the only thing he loved more than mussels was little children.

Kate managed to mumble, "Johnny, you're always spoiling things." She splashed water on him.

"Now guys, stop that! We've got a mission," Wendell said. "That's right!" Dale shouted as he led the way. Slowly, everyone followed.

At times, the water came up to their chins as they walked from reef to reef. When they came to the last reef, they quickly climbed out of the water and onto Cockroach Island. A loud noise came from the top of Abbot's Cliff. The children knew it was Kadova. Chills ran down the children's backs as they walked around Cockroach Island. To their surprise, they could find no bugs.

Dale spoke first. "It looks like the roaches have found another island."

Johnny brushed himself. "I still feel the chills that started when Kadova screamed."

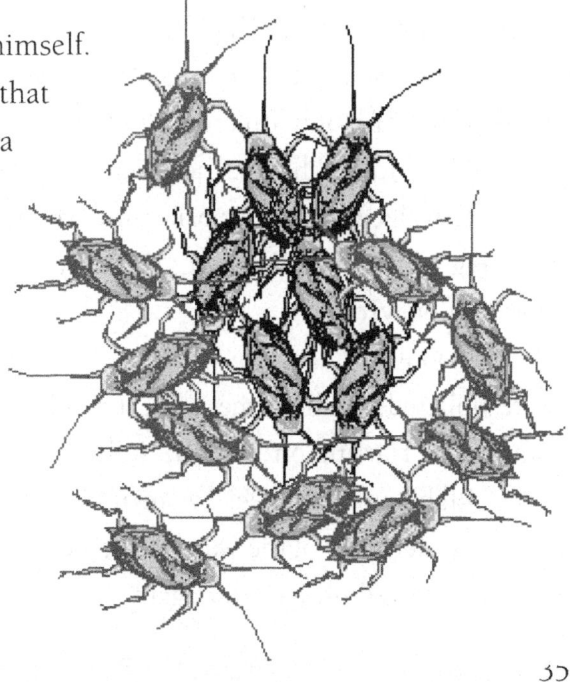

Kate shone her flashlight at Johnny, who jumped and let out a howl. He was covered with cockroaches. Everyone shone their flashlights at each other. They were all covered with roaches; thousands of roaches skittered all over the children. The weight dragged the children down to their knees, and then they lay flat on the ground.

The cockroaches crawled under the children and carried them to a big cave lit by the eyes of millions of cockroaches. The insects flapped their wings, and the loud hum deafened the children. The noise suddenly stopped, and all the cockroaches put the kids down and joined the other roaches.

The kids looked at each other. What was going to happen next? More chills ran down their backs.

The biggest cockroach they had ever dreamed of appeared in front of them. He was as big as they were. Big Roach asked, "What brings you little brats here?"

Kate told the roach about the big race. When she was finished, Big Roach angrily shouted, "That's all your kind think of us for — fun and games, and then you crush us. Well, we play a game, too. It's similar to yours. The only difference is that we get to eat the losers." He laughed. He ordered his roaches, "Take these kids to the far end of the cave." He walked to the opposite end. The roaches lined the kids up facing Big Roach, who shouted, "Get on your mark!"

The kids obeyed.

"Get set! Go!"

Kate hollered, "Follow me!" She ran like the wind, out of the cave and into Harrington Sound, followed close behind by the Invisibles. Right on their heels were millions of roaches. The kids swam underwater most of the way, and came up only for mouthfuls of air before they dived underwater again.

The Adventures of Eugene

When Kate reached Mussel Bay, followed closely by Wendell and Dale, she glanced over her shoulder. "Where's Johnny?"

Johnny screamed. Something pulled him under the water.

The children ran back to help. They swatted the air and fought their way through the cockroaches that flew all around them. They knew they could not save Johnny, and they would probably have a hard time saving themselves.

A loud clap of thunder rang out, followed by a flash of lightning that lit up the whole bay. All the roaches flew away. Eugene stood on the top of the water, holding the magic dagger high above his head. He put one hand into the water, and out popped Johnny. Eugene vanished, and the Invisibles, plus one girl, went home.

The next day, God's children met on the railway tracks with their roaches, big ones and little ones. The kids drew several long lines with sticks, then they put a roach in each line. When the race was about to start, Johnny noticed a big roach in Kate's hair. He snatched at it. Kate was about to slap Johnny, until he showed her the roach. Johnny placed the big roach in one of the lines, and the race began.

All the roaches ran toward the end, all except Kate's big roach, who just lay there. All of God's children laughed. Slowly, as everyone watched, the big roach swayed from side to side, then took off like a bullet, overtook all the other roaches, and crossed the finish line first.

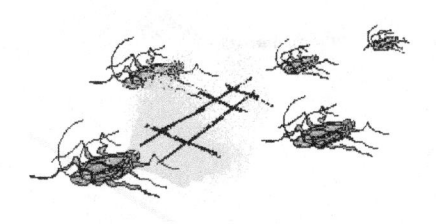

Kate and the Invisibles clapped with joy.

Rabbit Island

One day Wendell and Kate were looking for land crabs at the bottom of Abbot's Cliff. The crabs lived in holes hidden between the rocks along the shoreline. Kate bent closer to a hole, and instead of a land crab, a baby rabbit popped out. She was amazed by the rabbit's beauty. He was fluffy, with white hair and blue eyes. While she looked at the animal, Kate felt a force of energy she could not understand, almost as if the creature had some sort of magical power over her. Kate felt completely relaxed, and the rabbit stretched out his paws and said, "Hello, what's your name?"

Kate's eyes popped open wide. She ran off calling, "Wendell, Wendell, come quick, come quick!"

Wendell hurried over to Kate. "What's wrong?" he asked. "Look what I found. It's a rabbit that can talk!"

"Kate, it's impossible. He's only a rabbit."

The Adventures of Eugene

"No, no! Say something," Kate demanded, but the rabbit just stared at Wendell.

"Well, now that we've found him, what are we going to do with him?" Wendell asked.

"We can't possibly leave him here. He'll be all alone. Let's take him home," Kate suggested as she gazed into the animal's eyes.

Wendell chuckled. "What if he belongs to one of the killer rabbits that live on Rabbit Island?"

"That's impossible. Killer rabbits can't swim," Kate answered. Wendell picked up the baby. "OK, if you say so."

When Kate and Wendell got home, they found a box, put some hay into it, and laid the furry creature inside. After they fed him celery and made him comfortable, they joined Johnny and Dale, near Francis Patton School. The boys were skimming flat rocks across the surface of the water. Wendell told the boys about the rabbit, and Johnny teased Kate, "You shouldn't have taken that rabbit from Rabbit Island."

Kate grew angry and chased Johnny, who shouted, "Killer Rabbit!" as he ran down the railway tracks.

Dale joined in with the teasing. Kate began to cry.

Wendell comforted her. "Don't worry about them. Let's go and pick some carrots from Mrs. Caisey's garden for our new pet. I'll bet he'll like that."

After they pulled up a few vegetables, they made their way toward home. Dale and Johnny joined them and apologized to

Kate. When Kate and Wendell reached their house, Kate ran into her room and looked into the box. It was empty. "Wendell, he's gone!"

"Don't panic!" Wendell answered. "He can't be far. Let's look around."

The sun was going down over the horizon, and the sky was getting dark. The kids searched the house. They grabbed their flashlights and went outside, they looked everywhere and were about to give up their search for the new pet, when they saw him hopping toward them. Kate ran over and picked him up. Wendell offered the baby a carrot. The rabbit turned his head.

Johnny laughed. "What kind of rabbit refuses a carrot?"

Dale said, "I know." He reached out to pat the rabbit, and the rabbit bit his finger, jumped out of Kate's arms, and hopped down the railway tracks shouting, "Killer rabbit!"

Kate and the Invisibles could not believe what they had heard. Johnny yelled,

"What do we do, with that killer rabbit on the loose? God's children could be in danger."

Dale held his painful finger. "We've got to destroy him." Kate cried, "I don't want to hurt my baby rabbit."

Wendell put his arm around her. "Let's catch him and take him back to Rabbit Island."

Kate sniffed. "That's a good idea."

Johnny added, "Wendell, you came up with the idea. How do we catch a flesh-eating rabbit without getting eaten?"

Wendell whispered, "Gather around." He told them of his plan. Dale laughed. "Which one of us is going to be the bait?"

"I'll be the bait." Kate bubbled.

The Adventures of Eugene

"Okay," said Wendell. "Let's hurry; we haven't got much time." They got a box and ran along the railway tracks looking for the killer rabbit. They stopped for a moment, when several dogs ran toward them howling, frightened out of their wits. The kids hid in a nearby bush and watched. In the distance, they saw what had frightened the dogs. The killer rabbit hopped in their direction.

Wendell shouted, "Let's do it!"

Kate ran into the center of the railway track. The rabbit bounced right up to her and said, "Now what have we got here? It looks like filet mignon." He was about to jump on Kate, when the Invisibles leaped out and covered the killer rabbit with the box, trapping him.

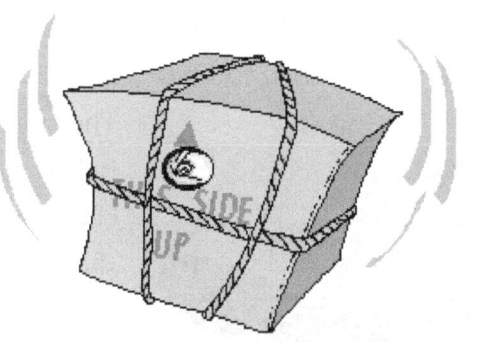

"We did it!" shouted the kids.

Dale said, "Let's get this bad boy back to Rabbit Island."

After tying up the box, they hurried to the school, where they crossed the road and entered Cherryland. The rabbit pleaded with Kate to set him free. As they passed Kadova's house, Kate stopped. "Do you think this is a good idea, taking him back to Rabbit Island? Listen to him. He sounds pitiful."

Johnny whispered, "Don't let him fool you." He pulled out a rubber finger and passed it to Kate.

She said, "OK, little rabbit, I'll set you free, if I'm sure you're not a killer rabbit."

The baby said, "I give you my word; I'm not a killer rabbit." Kate slowly inserted the finger in a hole in the box. "I told you he's not a killer rabbit," She told Johnny, but when she pulled out the finger, half of it was gone. Kate blurted out, "You lied to me!"

The rabbit said, "It only proves you can take a killer rabbit from Rabbit Island, but you can't take the killer out of the rabbit."

Dale nodded. "Are you satisfied?"

The group continued to Abbot's Cliff and climbed down the rocky path to the bottom. While they were swimming to Rabbit Island, the killer rabbit called out to Mussel Man for help. Johnny grew more frightened and tried to hold onto Kate. She told him to calm down.

The rabbit laughed at them. When the kids reached the island, they quickly climbed out of the water. Wendell shouted, "Cover your eyes, it's the giant turtle!" Eugene had warned them not to look into the eyes of the turtle, which was why they had never even gone near Turtle Island. When they finally uncovered their eyes, they saw that the box was opened, and the killer rabbit had escaped.

Johnny said, "Let's get out of here!" He was about to dive back into the water, when all around them, rabbits popped out of their holes. The kids shook and held onto each other. The rabbits hopped toward the children and made scraping noises with their teeth. Right before the animals attacked, the sky lit up. The killer rabbits turned and scurried back into their holes.

The light blinded the kids, but they recognized Eugene's voice. "You remembered what I told you about the giant turtle, and you covered your eyes," he said. "I'm proud of you." The voice stopped, and the light faded. The kids quickly swam back to land and made their way back home.

The next day Kate slept late. When she awoke, she saw a fluffy white rabbit lying beside her. She leaped out of bed.

The Invisibles, who were standing around her, all laughed. Wendell said, "We bought you a real rabbit."

Kate calmed down and picked up the rabbit. She looked into his eyes, and he winked his big blue eyes. Kate smiled at the Invisibles. "Thank you," she said.

Trunk Island

Early that morning, as David lay in his bed, he felt something crawling on his chest. He threw back the covers and found a mouse. He almost sprang out of bed, but stopped, when the mouse said, "Don't be afraid. My name is Klaus, and I have an urgent message from Eugene.

When Eugene was entering Atlantis, a wicked goblin stole the little glass bottle that entrapped the Russian wind. Without the Russian wind, Eugene cannot open the door to Atlantis to come out again. David, you must find the bottle and take it back to Atlantis."

David's fright subsided. "Where do I find this goblin? When I find the Russian wind, how do I get to Atlantis?"

Klaus answered, "The goblin lives on Trunk Island. Once you get the bottle, you must take it to Bay Island, at midnight, and bring all God's children with you." Klaus leapt to the floor and ran through a hole in the wall.

David slid out of bed and told all of God's children what Klaus had told him.

All day, the children prepared themselves. They rubbed oil on their bodies, so they would be slippery, if they were caught. They tied garlic cloves around their necks, to keep away vampires and evil spirits. They all found flashlights, because the rocky path that led to Abbot's Cliff was dark.

When evening finally arrived, all of God's children met on the railway track and wore red scarves around their heads. They rushed over to Francis Patton School, where they crossed the street to Cherryland. With all the flashlights on, they walked on the dark rocky path toward Abbot's Cliff. When they passed Kadova's house, they heard screams, but instead of running back home, they ran to Abbot's Cliff. When they reached the top, they looked across to Trunk Island, which they couldn't see well, because a mist covered it. Trunk Island was only about six acres big, in the center of Harrington Sound.

The Trinity Church bells gonged. The children shuddered and looked toward the east, beyond the cherry trees. They could see the cross of Trinity Church, and it glowed in the dark. They quickly scurried down the path that led to the bottom of Abbot's Cliff.

David said he had to go to Trunk Island alone, to get the Russian wind from the goblin. David jumped in and swam through the dark, lonely waters of Harrington Sound toward Trunk Island.

When David reached the island, he climbed out of the water to be greeted by the wicked goblin, who had a smile on his face. Tied around his neck was the little glass bottle that entrapped the Russian wind. His fingernails were a foot long. He gripped David and carried him back to his cave, where he tied David's arms and legs. The goblin sat on a nearby rock, pulled out a bottle of whiskey, and gulped it. After each big swallow, the goblin poked David with a long fingernail. When David pulled away, the goblin laughed. He continued to prod and push David until the whiskey was all gone. By that time, the goblin was so drunk, he fell off the rock, sound asleep.

David sobbed because he knew he could not free himself. Nearby, he heard a noise. He found Klaus, the mouse, nibbling at the rope. "Hurry!" David whispered, and soon the little rodent freed David.

Klaus scuttled over to the goblin and nibbled at the rope around his neck that held the little glass bottle containing the Russian wind. When he finally cut through that rope, he dragged the bottle over to David. David thanked the mouse, took the bottle, ran out of the cave, and jumped into Harrington Sound. He swam toward God's children, who shone their flashlights, so David could see.

David was about 100 yards from God's children, when he heard a loud screech coming from Trunk Island. It was the goblin, who Jumped into the water and was swimming fiercely toward David. God's children heard the angry bellows from the goblin as he got closer to David. The children shouted to David to hurry up, but he could not out-swim the goblin. Soon he felt sharp fingernails on the back of his feet, as he swam for his life.

To make things worse, a loud noise issued forth from the top of Abbot's Cliff. David and all of God's children knew it was Kadova, who jumped off the high cliff and landed on top of the goblin and wrestled him to the bottom of Harrington Sound.

When David reached God's children, they said he had only fifteen minutes left before midnight. They all quickly climbed up the cliff and ran along the rocky path. When they reached the end, they crossed the road, passed Francis Patton School, made their way down the railway track, hurried to the Walker house, and crossed over the water. Twenty-five yards of it were shallow enough to walk through, but fifty yards of deep water remained, before they reached their island. Before them, three big manta rays flapped their mighty wings and swung their deadly tails from side to side. One of God's children exclaimed, "What do we do now? We've only got two minutes left."

David took the red scarf from around his head and tied it around his flashlight, so that it glowed red. He raised the flashlight high in the air. The manta rays thought he was Eugene with the magic dagger.

They quickly swam away.

All of God's children swam swiftly to Bay Island, where Klaus met them and said, "Quick, follow me." He ran to the top of Bay Island. When they reached the peak, Klaus told them to make a circle around David and hold their flashlights above their heads. "The Russian wind cannot pass through light," said the little creature, " and you must release the wind and recapture it. Hurry! You've only got thirty seconds."

David uncorked the small bottle, and out rushed the Russian wind, swirling around, trying to escape the circle of lights. It blew David off his feet. Klaus rushed over. "Get up! Hurry!"

David struggled to his feet, still holding the bottle high in the air. The bottle sucked the Russian wind back in with a horrendous swirling sound. David quickly pressed the cork back onto the bottle, and the noise ceased. Not for long, though, because the island trembled like an earthquake and cracked in half.

Klaus said, "You must jump into the big opening." Without hesitation, holding the glass bottle in his hand, David walked to the edge and dropped in. The crack closed over him, as if nothing had never happened.

All of God's children were speechless. A flash of lightning lit up the sky, and a flight of golden stairs descended from the heavens. David walked down the stairs. In another flash of lightning, Eugene stood at the top of the stairs holding the magic dagger high above his head.

All God's children applauded with joy.

Made in United States
Orlando, FL
13 November 2024